Based on the chorus of "Buffalo Gals," originally published in 1844

Dance by the

For dear Kathy Yep, with a
lighthearted step. May you dance
by the light of the moon!
—J.R.

For Rick and Amy
—G.F.

For information address Hyperion Books for Children,

114 Fifth Avenue, New York, New York 10011-5690.

Printed in Singapore · First Edition · 1 3 5 7 9 10 8 6 4 2 · Designed by Elizabeth H. Clark

This book is set in Bembo.

Library of Congress Cataloging-in-Publication Data on file. ISBN 0-7868-1820-4 · Reinforced binding

Visit www.hyperionbooksforchildren.com

Light of the Moon

WRITTEN BY **Joanne Ryder**
ILLUSTRATED BY **Guy Francis**

HYPERION BOOKS FOR CHILDREN
NEW YORK

Buffalo Flo
has an elegant bow,
a grand sash that flows
from her head to her toes.

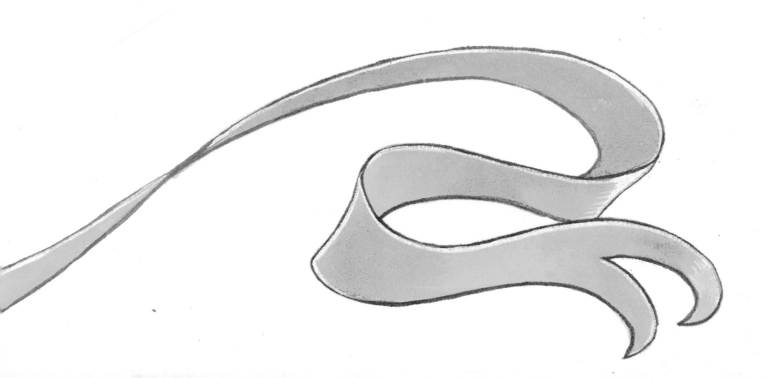

In her bow, light and loose,
lovely Flo calls to Goose:
"*A dance by the light of the moon!*"

Gertie May Goose
sports a new pair of shoes,
with rap-tapping taps
and crisscrossing straps.

In her snazzy black flats,
Gertie May honks to Cat:

Cassie Sue Cat
dons her flip-floppy hat,
drifting flowers and lace.
What style! What grace!
With a flourish and jig,
Cassie Sue purrs to Pig:

Patty Ann Pig
picks the prettiest wig,
and her long silky curls
float around as she twirls.
Patty Ann joins her pals,
and she oinks to the gals:

"Let's dance by the light of the moon!"

Gals from the farm
stroll on by, arm in arm.
They glide to the glen,
but . . . where are the men?
How could they be late
for a toe-tapping date:
Come dance by the light of the moon!

Buddies and boys,
show yourselves, make some noise!
These gals are a sight,
and the mood feels just right.
Hey, boys, don't waste time
when the evening is fine
for a dance by the light of the moon!

Here are the guys!
They're in trousers and TIES!
They've got flowers in hand,
and they look really grand!

Gentle guys, you've done great.
Now, sweet gals, pick your date
and dance by the light of
the moon.

"I've got my banjo,"
yells old Farmer Snow.
"Gals and guys, give a cheer
now that everyone's here!

"It's a party for YOU:
For my friends, good and true!

"*Go dance by the light of the moon!*"

They danced . . .

by the light . . .

Based on the chorus of "Buffalo Gals," originally published in 1844

Oh! Buf - fa - lo gals, will you come out to-night, will you come out to-night, will you come out to-night,